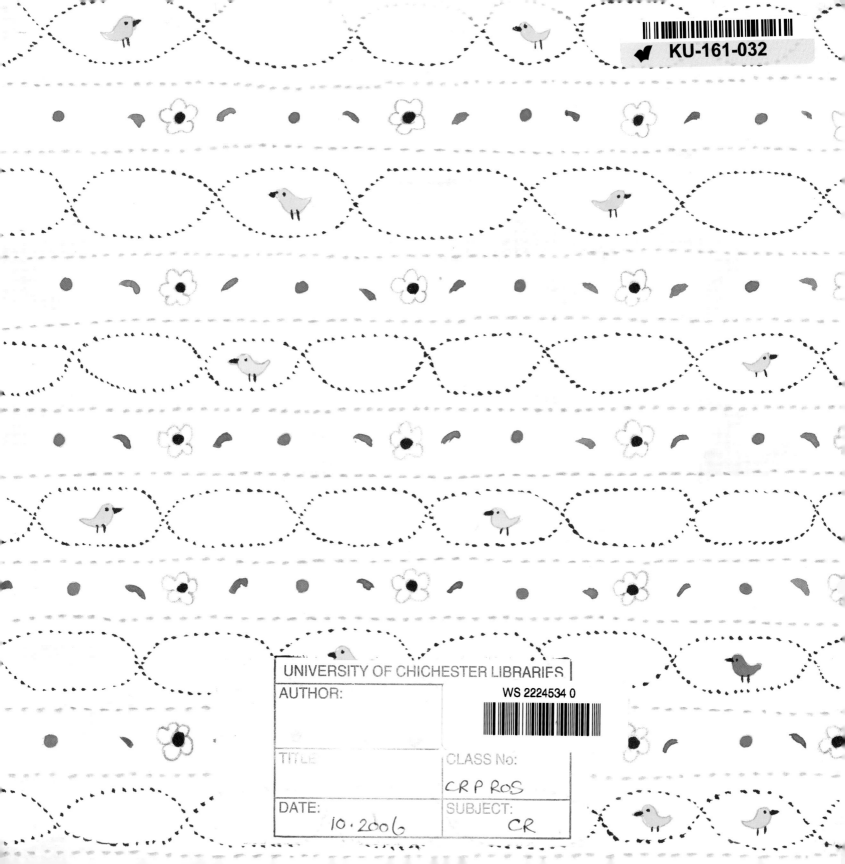

For Elsie and Emile ~ M·R.   For my Mum ~ C.L.

First published 2006 by Walker Books Ltd
87 Vauxhall Walk, London SE11 5HJ

10 9 8 7 6 5 4 3 2 1

Text © 2006 Michael Rosen
Illustrations © 2006 Chinlun Lee

The right of Michael Rosen and Chinlun Lee to be identified as author and illustrator respectively of
this work has been asserted by them in accordance with the Copyright, Designs and Patents Act 1988

This book has been typeset in GillSans Light

Printed in China

Lindy   Nicole   Molly   Russell

British Library Cataloguing in Publication Data:
a catalogue record for this book is available from the British Library

ISBN-13: 978-0-7445-6182-1
ISBN-10: 0-7445-6182-5

www.walkerbooks.co.uk   www.michaelrosen.co.uk

Totally Wonderful
Miss Plumberry

Michael Rosen

illustrated by Chinlun Lee

WALKER BOOKS
AND SUBSIDIARIES
LONDON · BOSTON · SYDNEY · AUCKLAND

It was a totally wonderful day.

Totally wonderful weather. Totally wonderful everything.

And today Molly was taking her crystal to school.

It came from the rocks at the back of Grandma's house.

Grandma over the water and far away gave it specially to Molly,

and only Molly …

Molly's own crystal that she kept by the side
of her bed so that she could look deep into it
as she was going to sleep.

At school Molly kissed

her mummy goodbye,

hung up her jacket

and ran

into the classroom.

Miss Plumberry was there
but she was talking
to Russell. Molly held
her crystal in her hands.

"Great crystal you've got there, Molly," said Tania.

"I love your crystal, Molly," said Lindy.

"Can I hold it, Molly?" asked Aaron.

"Me first, Molly,"
said Nicole.

Everyone crowded around Molly and her crystal.
Tania and Lindy and Aaron and Nicole
and Zak and Madeleine and Jamie.

Everyone wanted to touch Molly's crystal.

Molly took in a breath and opened her mouth:

"This crystal comes from my grandma over—"

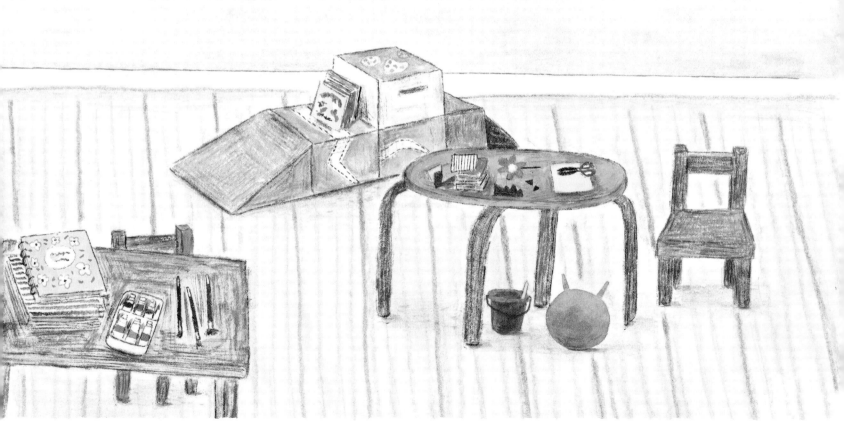

But just then Russell ran past waving
a pink and green dinosaur.

"It's a stegosaurus," he said.

"It's got twenty spikes and if you
press it here it spurts water."

And everyone said, "Wow!"

They forgot about Molly and her crystal
from Grandma and crowded
around Russell instead.

Molly's eyes went hot and wet.

She looked at her crystal lying snug in her hand.

She felt her heart go

thumpity-thumpity-thumpity inside.

It wasn't a totally wonderful day.

It was a totally horrible day.

The most totally horrible day
in the whole world.

And in a minute a great big lion was going
to run in and gobble everyone up.

Come on lion,

come on lion,

thought Molly.

Just then Miss Plumberry looked up.

She saw everyone crowded around Russell.

She saw Molly all by herself.

She saw Molly looking sad.

"Molly, what have you got there?" she asked.

Molly said, "It's my crystal from Grandma.

But nobody likes it except me."

Miss Plumberry stood very still.
Then she clapped her hands and
everyone looked at her.

"Molly," said Miss Plumberry,

"tell me about this crystal."

Molly said,

"It's my crystal from Grandma over the water and far away and it comes from the rocks at the back of her house and I keep it by the side of my bed so I can look deep into it as I'm going to sleep."

Miss Plumberry looked at the crystal very, very closely.

Then she said,

"Molly, your crystal is totally wonderful.

It's one of the most lovely and perfect things

I've ever seen.

"When I look into it,
it feels like I'm falling and falling
and falling deep into a warm pool.

And I look and I look and I look some more,

and then it feels like it's looking back at me."

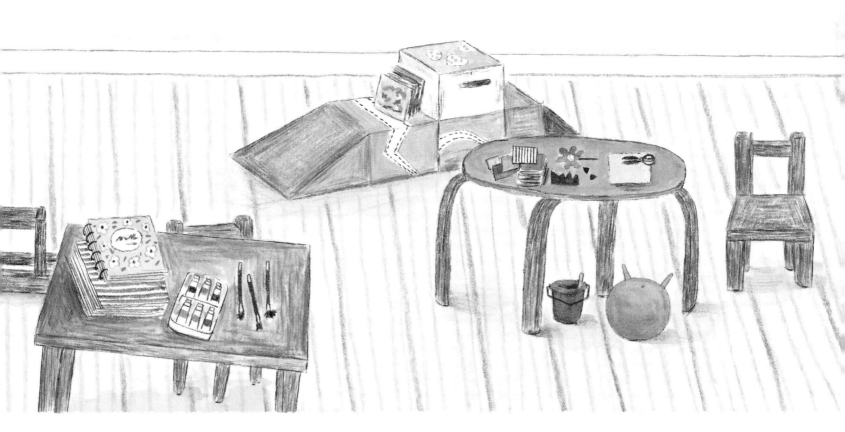

After that everyone wanted to look into Molly's crystal.

"Can I hold it?" asked Russell.

"Can I?" said Nicole.

"Then me," said Lindy.

"And me," said Aaron.

Maybe it's not the most totally horrible day, Molly thought. Maybe it's the most totally wonderful day. And Miss Plumberry is the most totally wonderful teacher in the whole world.

Totally wonderful Miss Plumberry.

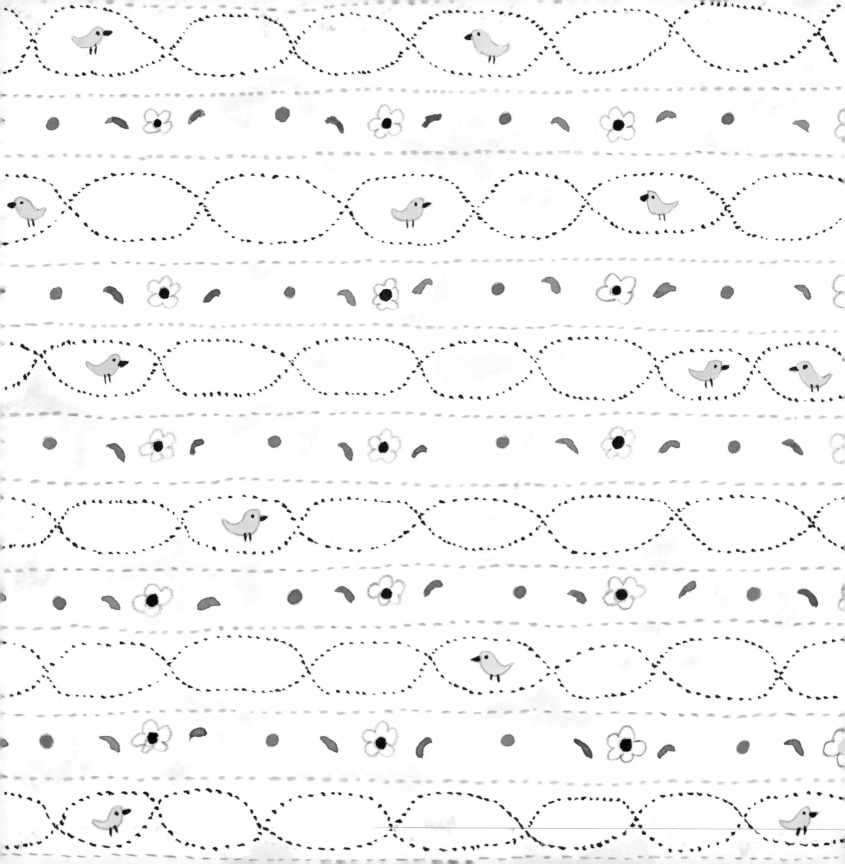